Bird Lady Meets Mort and Ort In "It's a Great Day for Grocery Shopping!"

To Autumn!
Be Well!
Gramma Golden
12/8/2021

Gramma Golden

authorHOUSE

AuthorHouse™
1663 Liberty Drive
Bloomington, IN 47403
www.authorhouse.com
Phone: 833-262-8899

Published by AuthorHouse 11/23/2021

ISBN: 978-1-6655-4503-7 (sc)
ISBN: 978-1-6655-4502-0 (e)

Library of Congress Control Number: 2021923708

Print information available on the last page.

Any people depicted in stock imagery provided by Getty Images are models, and such images are being used for illustrative purposes only. Certain stock imagery © Getty Images.

This book is printed on acid-free paper.

Because of the dynamic nature of the Internet, any web addresses or links contained in this book may have changed since publication and may no longer be valid. The views expressed in this work are solely those of the author and do not necessarily reflect the views of the publisher, and the publisher hereby disclaims any responsibility for them.

Bird Lady had just handed the flight attendant Ebenezer, her giraffe look-alike walking stick, to put in the storage closet. She then took her place in window Seat G1 on the airplane that would finally take her back to her home town. Her seat felt a bit tight so she raised the armrest of Seat G2 to give her more room, hoping no one was assigned to that seat on the flight home.

She very much enjoyed her winter vacation away from home this year spending it in warmer weather at the beach, but she was ready to head back to tend to her gardens once spring arrived. She knew it was several weeks away as the cold weather was not yet gone. *It's a good thing I packed warm clothes for the flight home*, she declared to herself as she sat there in her maroon corduroy pants, long sleeved floral patterned turtle neck shirt, blue down vest and brown tie shoes.

While looking out the small window of the airplane, her thoughts wandered to the last time she flew in a plane with Pete the Pilot. She pictured in her mind the beautiful clean beach and ocean water filled with lovely sea creatures as she and Pete flew over water's edge below. Trailing behind them was the banner reminding beach goers to discard trash in proper containers. Bird Lady was happy that Pete the Pilot promised to continue to fly the banner behind his plane weekly in order to remind people to keep beaches litter free.

As the flight attendant's announcement was made, awakening Bird Lady from her thoughts, it was time to fasten her seatbelt and prepare for takeoff. After several attempts and continued struggles, Bird Lady finally buckled her belt. *Oh my,* she thought to herself, *have they made these belts shorter or have I gotten bigger?* It would be a four hour flight home and Bird Lady knew she wouldn't unbuckle her belt to go through that again!

Once they were in the air, she took a book out of her green palm tree leaf design on yellow straw carry-on bag. She started to read but her mind drifted back to the beach. She remembered her excitement over meeting her friends, Mort and Ort Aahkamort, while they relaxed in their beach chairs. She fondly thought of when they all came up with a plan to get beach goers to help keep beaches clean. And sadly, she thought of the day Mort and Ort suddenly disappeared, wondering if they would ever meet again.

Bird Lady looked down at her orange oversized wristwatch she bought as a souvenir on the beach that had blue and grey dancing dolphins on the wide band. She was hoping more flight time had passed as she sensed she was getting more uncomfortable from the tight seatbelt. Her thoughts again drifted to all the wonderful restaurants she ate at while on vacation. Crab rolls, lobster bisque soup, burgers, steaks, chops and lobster tails with drawn butter. *No wonder this belt is tight!* she thought. She was certain it was weight gain and vowed to do a much better job of choosing what to eat when she got home.

G1

As expected, the flight home was on time. She arranged for assistance from the gate at the airport and was thankful, even though she had Ebenezer by her side, she didn't have to walk the long hallways to get her luggage. After all, her shoes felt tight from sitting so long and would hurt if she walked any distance. Hmmm, she wondered, *did my feet gain weight too?* she chuckled with concern.

Finally home, her neighbor Nellie called out to her from across the street as she arrived. She spent the next ten minutes chatting with Nellie, giving her a quick recap of her weeks away at the beach. Since Nellie was wearing only a green short sleeved house dress and no jacket, she was ready to go inside to warm up from the chilly air. Bird Lady had a lot to do so she was okay with their ten minute chat. She wasn't able to talk to Nellie's husband Norman yet about the birds so would do that next time. He kindly offered to keep Bird Lady's bird feeders full of nuts and seeds while she vacationed. She couldn't wait to talk to him to see how they all did in the cold weather.

Bird Lady decided to unpack her luggage first and then write a shopping list. The pantry, refrigerator and freezer were nearly empty since she didn't want anything to spoil while she was gone. She knew it would take quite a bit of time to shop so she decided to go first thing in the morning. After a long day of travel, she rested that evening in her royal blue and white snowflake patterned flannel nightgown. She drifted off to sleep under a cozy comforter in her rocking chair in front of her fireplace, dreaming of her, Ebenezer, Mort and Ort walking along the beach.

The next morning, she dressed in her once very comfortable purple sweat suit, noticing it too was a bit tight. She vowed she would learn to eat the right kinds of food in the right amounts by the time the garden needed attention.

But where would she begin? She already spent a lifetime losing weight and gaining it right back. Even as a child she remembers being teased and bullied about her size. She wasn't good at sports and didn't exercise much so she spent a lot of time alone. She knew she had to make good food choices now and decided to start right away.

She drove to the local grocer early that day with her shopping list and pencil in her pink and grey striped shoulder bag. It was a very lovely but chilly day. The sun was shining in the beautiful blue sky. She couldn't help but think to herself 'It's a great day for grocery shopping!'

She parked the car, took Ebenezer out, took a grocery cart from the cart corral placing Ebenezer in the basket and walked in the automatic door. She hadn't shopped much while on vacation, mostly eating out at restaurants. The store was very large and would require a lot of walking so Bird Lady was wearing her white and turquois athletic shoes that felt tighter than usual.

Once she passed the checkout counter, she was in the vegetable aisle. She couldn't help but notice how colorful the fresh vegetables looked. She usually chose frozen vegetables with butter or cheese sauce. But today, she was committed to make good choices.

As the warning bell chimed, the fresh water sprayer began to spread a clean mist onto the vegetables, keeping them fresh for shoppers. It was at the same time through the foggy mist that Bird Lady suddenly spotted two tall, colorful birds with tie dyed feathers pushing a shopping cart together, side by side. *It can't be! But it is! It's Mort and Ort Aahkamort shopping in the same place at the same time as me!*, she exclaimed to herself.

She called out "Hey, it's me! Bird Lady! Over here! I am over here!" waving with delight. They both turned and looked at her with their large brown eyes and a huge grin on their beaks when they recognized her voice and spotted her.

Moving swiftly toward one another, Bird Lady couldn't wait for their hugs. As their colorful tie-dyed wings enveloped her, Mort announced "Looks like your face is a bit fuller. You ate well there at the beach, huh?" Right away, he realized how rude that comment must have sounded and knew he owed her an apology. "Please forgive me for being so rude." Changing the subject quickly, Mort said "It's really great to see you again. We've missed you."

Immediately, Ort tried to shush him with her raised eyebrow look but with no luck. She invited Bird Lady to join them in the grocer's coffee shop to sit and chat awhile about her vacation. She gladly accepted .

They chose a small table in the back of the shop. Bird Lady knew no one else could see her friends and didn't want others to think she was talking to herself. With her back to the cashier, Bird Lady excitedly gave updates about seeing less trash on the beach after Mort and Ort disappeared that day. She also told them Pete the Pilot promised he would fly his plane and banner weekly over the water's edge as a reminder to beach goers to put trash in proper containers.

After a while and with no further updates to share, Bird Lady decided to revisit Mort's comment about her fuller face. "You were right, Mort," she responded. "My face isn't the only thing fuller. My seat and seat belt on the plane were tight as were my shoes," she sadly admitted. "I have to do something to lose this weight and do it fast! After all, I'm not getting any younger," she said with the sadness still in her voice.

"Losing weight fast is not healthy, plus you'll only gain it right back," Ort commented with confidence. Mort spoke up next. "According to many experts, losing 1-2 pounds each week is a healthy and safe rate. More than that can put you at risk of many other problems including muscle loss."

"You're right," Bird Lady answered looking down at her ample belly. "But I've tried to lose weight since I was a child and just cannot keep it off. I remember getting bullied and teased at school and being called names and made fun of." Ort noticed Bird Lady's eye spill over a tear as she spoke.

"Childhood obesity is a major health concern," remarked Ort. "Statistics show that obesity affects 1 in 5 children in the United States. It can be less though through proper education, healthy eating and regular physical activity."

"Come to think of it," piped up Bird Lady, "I've read where places have set up walking trails or paths to be used by anyone to get some outdoor exercise. I'll have to try that. I'm sure Ebenezer wouldn't mind a change of scenery," she winked.

"Shopping malls and school facilities open early, too, for the public to use indoors to get exercise safely or during bad weather!" Ort exclaimed.

Mort added "Many communities offer classes on losing weight in healthy ways too. Places like early childhood centers, hospitals, schools and food service have lots to offer in teaching children and adults about obesity and weight control."

"Setting up healthy food environments is also helpful," Ort continued. "Supermarkets, fast food chains, restaurants and even farmers markets now place nutrition and calorie count information in full view for customers to see."

Mort spoke up next. "Better yet, certain standards to follow are set up for childcare, schools, hospitals and workplaces. For example, schools can encourage drinking water instead of sugar sweetened beverages while encouraging children to eat food like fruits, vegetables, whole grains and nonfat or low-fat dairy products."

Knowingly, Ort professed "According to experts on the internet site www.myplate.gov, a good food plan is based on age, sex, height, weight and physical activity." She continued, "Servings for fruit vary between 1 to 2 cups each day, vegetables between 1 and 3 cups each day. Grains like bread, cereal, rice and pasta should be at least half whole wheat. Proteins such as seafood, meat, poultry, eggs, and nuts should amount to between 2 and 6 ½ ounces each day. And finally, the dairy group includes milk, yogurt, and cheese and are recommended to be low-fat and from 1 ½ to 3 cups each day. Nutrition labels on the food should be checked for serving sizes too," she concluded.

"You're right!" joined in Bird Lady. "I remember looking at the nutrition label on my 24-ounce bottle of sweetened soda and saw there were three servings in the bottle! I have been drinking the entire bottle on my own!"

Mort smirked, saying, "I'd be as big as that plane you flew in over the beach if I ate that much food each and every day!" Ort kindly reminded him he's a bird and he eats like a bird. Suddenly, Bird Lady laughed out loud, causing the cashier to look her way, obviously wondering why she was laughing like that with no one else at her table. Embarrassed by that, Bird Lady settled down.

Changing topics, Mort commented on the need for some form of daily physical activity. "Walking is a great way to get the proper amount of physical activity recommended by experts which is at least 150 minutes every week. That's about 20-25 minutes each day. Plus it costs nothing to take a walk every day nor does it require any special skills or equipment. Except maybe the cost of a walking stick like Ebenezer," he said with a chuckle.

Ort chimed in, saying "Plus you get the benefit of sleeping better, improve your ability to think, learn and improve your memory."

"I can certainly use that!" Bird Lady noted with a wink. "My doctor told me walking can also lower the chances of getting heart disease, cancer and diabetes."

"That goes for children too," Ort said knowingly. "Nowadays, children have too many things to do that require no real physical activity such as watching TV or playing games on their phone or notepad or television. Doing that and sitting for hours can lead to weight gain. Experts say that children and teens should have 60 minutes of physical activity every day between physical education classes, recess, classroom based activity and other out-of-school activities."

"Having healthy choices available at school and home is important," spoke up Mort. "But it starts with teaching what exactly a healthy food choice is."

"I know many of my choices are not so healthy," admitted Bird Lady. "Sweets are my weakness like sweetened sodas, ice cream, desserts and candy. I also buy salty food for snacks like nuts and chips and of course dips to go with them. And I don't eat many vegetables."

"It's okay and can be fun to eat those kinds of items in moderation, like say when you visit Gramma's house, right?" Mort chuckled.

"Right! And many schools have changed their food choices and have limited but healthy items in vending machines," Ort commented. "Many have had students, parents, community members and teachers get together to set up better eating and physical activity opportunities."

"Like what?" inquired Bird Lady.

"Like opening up gymnasiums and weight equipment rooms at school for the community and students," Ort continued. "Like adding outdoor activity time as part of the daily routine. Like not tolerating teasing or bullying someone because of their weight."

Please Discar
Waste in Prope
Containers

REPORT CARD

"Bullying leads to sadness and feeling alone," Bird Lady disclosed with a look of sadness on her face. "I remember being teased because I couldn't run very fast and I couldn't tumble in gym class. I never used the monkey bars on the school playground because my arms couldn't hold me up. Getting on the teeter-totter was useless....I always bottomed out! Mostly, I was embarrassed, too, on days at school when the gym teacher weighed and measured us and wrote it on our report card."

Bird Lady continued. "I didn't like being on teams, either, because I was always the last one chosen by the team captain. I knew they were whispering about me.....'Don't pick her! She can't run!'" they would laughingly say. I never went to summer camp either because I looked too big in a bathing suit. The other kids would make fun of me."

"That's just not right," Ort vocalized firmly. "People need to understand what bullying does to someone's feelings. It's hurtful!"

Mort knowingly added "It's a fact that bullying of children and teens causes depression, stress and damage to self-esteem, or how they feel about themselves. And that can lead to overeating. It's a vicious circle."

"Bullying isn't only name calling. Some bullies would even push me or trip me and make up lies about me," admitted Bird Lady as she vividly remembered those times on the playground. "And nowadays," she continued, "children are bullied on social media sites where bullies write and share negative, harmful, false or mean things about others. That makes me so sad!"

Mort spoke up. "Children need to treat others with kindness and care for others no matter what. They need to accept others as they are."

Bird Lady added, "I wonder what I can do now that I'm old to help people understand that bullying and teasing is not acceptable and it only makes matters worse."

"You're never too old!" Ort uttered with authority. "But let's start with you getting healthier and then maybe you'll figure out what you can do later."

"I know where we can start," proposed Mort. "I heard that if you do your grocery shopping by going only around the outer aisles of the grocery store, that's where the healthy choices are. Some inner aisles are okay too for choosing cereals, rice and pasta. But most inner aisles are where the foods you crave are that are less healthy. Let's go see for ourselves!"

"That's a great idea! Let's go shopping together! After all, it's a great day for grocery shopping!" Bird Lady offered with excitement for trying her new way of shopping. All three jumped up from the table as Bird Lady gripped her grocery cart with Ebenezer still waiting patiently in the basket. Then they headed toward the first section of their adventure..... the bread aisle.

Bird Lady was tickled she had Mort and Ort on each side of her as she walked through the bread section. "Now don't forget that we need to find whole wheat, oat or grain bread," voiced Ort. "White bread is not as good for you"

Bird Lady was amazed at all the different choices, including donuts, coffee cakes, cupcakes and other sweets she noticed in the bread section. While they were tempting, she quietly thought to herself, *I'll have these for special occasions!* as she walked right past them with a smile on her face.

"Next up, fresh vegetables and fruit," shouted Mort, startling Bird Lady from her thoughts, as if he knew what she was thinking.

Bird Lady was in awe just looking at the beautiful assortment of colors, shapes and sizes in this section. Bright red apples, stunningly orange oranges, greenish yellow bananas, pears, hairy kiwi, purple plums, strawberries, raspberries, green, red and black seedless grapes all looked better than usual to her this time. Vine ripened red tomatoes, leafy lettuce, dark green cucumbers, broccoli in bunches, bumpy heads of cauliflower and bright orange carrots all seemed to draw her to their beauty. She placed what she needed in her basket next to Ebenezer and marched off to the next outer aisle section behind with Mort and Ort leading the way.

"I see this section has frozen turkey and fish followed by fresh meat in the coolers ahead," declared Ort. "We must find chicken and the other white meat, pork, as well." As they strolled, Bird Lady added a frozen turkey breast, skinless chicken breasts, pork tenderloin, fresh salmon, shrimp and tilapia to her basket.

"Before we go any further, I see the aisle with brown rice and pasta choices," Mort pointed. "Cereals can't be that far either. We need to choose unsweetened cereals that have whole grains like barley corn, rice, rye and oats." It took a while for Bird Lady to choose her pasta and cereal, but she finally added to her cart the items Mort suggested she buy. It was helpful looking at the food nutrition labels to help her choose.

Next, they headed back to the outer aisle that shelved the dairy products. Bird Lady continued to look for and found low-fat yogurt, cottage cheese, cheese and milk. *Eggs are a good choice too,* she thought, adding them to her cart.

"Next stop.....frozen foods!" blurted Mort as he pretended to shiver.

"Just be sure to look for frozen vegetables without all the sauces and butter mixed in," noted Ort. "Too many fats and calories in them. Frozen yogurt for a treat at night is okay too," Ort giggled as she saw the ice cream section up ahead. Bird Lady complied with her by choosing frozen raspberry yogurt while looking away from the exceptionally long case of ice cream choices she passed by.

"Our last and final corner to turn before we head to the cashier," bellowed Mort. "Remember, no sweetened drinks for you unless it's for a special occasion when we all three will share the 24-ounce bottle!"

"I guess that means no sugar added water, tea or juice either unless it's for a special occasion," Bird Lady agreed.

Ort asked "But did you know that a fizzy water that has natural flavoring from limes, lemons or berries is a better choice and so crisp and refreshing?"

"Yes, water is important for good health. Experts recommend you drink eight 8-ounce glasses of water each day," Bird Lady noted.

As Mort gazed at her grocery cart full of good, nutritious food choices, he proclaimed to Bird Lady, "I'll bet you'll be surprised that this basketful of food will cost you less than normal. When you choose chips, crackers, dips, cookies, candy, pizza and other prepared packaged goods, your bill only gets bigger."

"And I get bigger too!" admitted Bird Lady as all three burst into laughter. Bird Lady was thrilled when she found that her basket of healthy goodies cost less as the cashier rang up the total.

Her shopping mission completed, Bird Lady walked toward the exit doors with Mort and Ort at her side and Ebenezer in her basket filled with grocery bags. With excitement and confidence in her voice, Bird Lady exclaimed to Mort and Ort as they strolled to her car, "You know, I have finally figured out what I can do with all this information you taught me now that I am old! I can write an educational children's book that reminds children and adults of our responsibility to help improve the health and well-being of upcoming generations. And then I can sell them at the Farmers Markets I go to in the summer!"

But by the time she finished her sentence, Mort and Ort had disappeared from her sides. She looked frantically up and down the rows of cars but could not find either one even as tall and colorful as they are. While she was saddened by their disappearance, Bird Lady was certain they knew she would carry on.

Welcome Gramma

And carry on she did indeed. She got home by noon, put her groceries away and fixed herself a healthy lunch from her new food choices. When she finished eating, she sat down in her cushioned brown leather office chair at her walnut brown wooden desk. She turned on her laptop computer sitting on her desk by the window. Facing out the window towards her back yard was a great way to watch the birds at the feeder while she thought about what to write.

And so she began:

Bird Lady had just handed the flight attendant Ebenezer, her giraffe look-alike walking stick, to put in the storage closet. She then took her place in window Seat G1 on the airplane that would finally take her back to her home town. Her seat felt a bit tight so she raised the armrest of Seat G2 to give her more room, hoping no one was assigned to that seat on the flight home.